The Fawn's Gift
retold by Lowell Morrison
illustrated by Deborah Healy

Text copyright © 1995 by Lowell Morrison
Illustrations copyright © 1995 by Deborah Healy
Designed by Russ Maselli

Published in 1995 by American Editions
150 East Wilson Bridge Road
Suite 145
Columbus, Ohio, 43085, USA

American Editions is an imprint of American Education Publishing Co.

ISBN 1-56189-396-X
Printed in the United States of American

the fawn's gift

—————————— A Lakota Legend ——————————

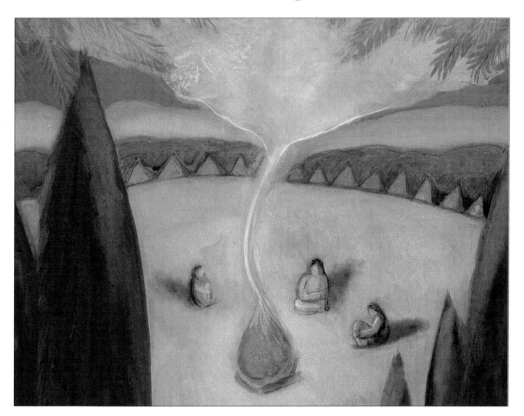

Retold by Lowell Morrison ➥ **Illustrated by Deborah Healy**

American Editions • Columbus • Ohio

Around a campfire that is now many years cold, in a village that is now many years gone, a child who is now many years grown asked this question, "Why teacher, does my brother run so swiftly while I run so slowly?"

"It is good you ask this," the teacher replied. "To answer, I will give you a gift — a gift of a story, a story about many gifts." And, for the child, he told this story, a story as old as earth itself.

From the fires, from the earth, from the water, from the sky, Wakan Tanka formed many creatures and many things in the early days. Wakan Tanka is our father. He is the father of the bear and the elm. He is the father of the fawn and the fox. He is the Great Mystery. He is the Great Maker. Wakan Tanka made all creatures a long time ago.

Often, Wakan Tanka would walk across the prairies, among the woods and through the mountains to look upon all that he made.

As he walked and saw those creatures he had already formed, he would think of new things to make. Sometimes he would add color. He would look at the gray fox and then make a fox of red. Other times, he would cut and trim the leaves of trees with his knife and tomahawk, making each a new kind. On one, he would push its roots deep in the dry lands so that they could find water. On another, he would spread the roots flat so that it would stand better on rocky slopes. In this way, he made many things, each suited to its own place.

Sometimes he would talk to himself or smile and laugh as he watched the creatures he had made enjoy the life he had given them. Sometimes he would talk to them as he walked along.

On one such walk, Bear, our brother, lumbered towards Wakan Tanka. Bear rose on his rear legs and towered over Wakan Tanka. "Thank you," Bear said, "for giving me such strength and size. I and others of my kind can move logs and dig up the earth to find what we eat. Thank you, Wakan Tanka."

Wakan Tanka laughed. "It is good you are happy. Your joy makes me happy, too! Live well, Bear!"

In the shadows, our brother Wolf bounced and dodged. He nipped playfully at Wakan Tanka's robe. "Thank you," said Wolf. "You have made my tribe swift and wise for the hunt."

"This, too, is good. Hunt well, Wolf!" said Wakan Tanka.

Robin flew about Wakan Tanka's head and then perched on his hand. "Thank you, Wakan Tanka, for giving me flight. Now I can fly from place to place in search of my dinner. And I can fly to the tops of the trees and rest safely from all danger."

"Rest well, Robin," said Wakan Tanka. He walked on and spoke aloud. "It is good what I have given Bear, Wolf, and Robin."

"It is good that Armadillo has his tough skin, Cougar has his sharp claws, and Ram has his great horns. It is good that Squirrel can leap from tree to tree and Eagle can soar in my heavens. All this is good. Each creature has a different gift, a gift that gives them an equal chance at life. It is good!"

As Wanka Tanka started to walk on, he heard a sound behind him. "What of my fawn, Wakan Tanka? What of him?" demanded Mother Deer as she stepped from the trees. Behind her stood little Fawn, weak and wobbly.

Wakan Tanka stopped and said, "I have given your tribe great speed. To your warriors, I have given sharp hooves and antlers. Is this not enough for Fawn as well?"

"I must leave Fawn when I graze. He is too weak to keep up and he is too wobbly to run if danger comes. He must stay behind, but our enemies can see him in the bushes. They can smell his scent. What chance has he against, Wolf, Coyote, and Cougar? What chance has he to live, Wakan Tanka?"

"This is not good!" shouted Wakan Tanka. "A tribe cannot exist without children. As I have changed Fox and the trees, I will change Fawn as well. What I have made, I can make better."

Wakan Tanka caught a cloud with his fingers and drew from it the color white. Then, he crushed a sandy stone in his fist.

He wetted both cloud and stone with water from the stream. In a great hollow stump, he mixed cloud and stone together. From Earth and Sky, he brought forth the colors white and tan.

Holding the colors, he stretched forth his hands over Fawn. First, Wanka Tanka

lightened Fawn's coat of tan. Next, he drew white spots and lines over it. As he

worked, Fawn seemed to disappear into the brush, into the trees, into the leaves

and tall grass until he could hardly be seen at all.

Wakan Tanka blew upon Fawn to dry the colors.

"Now it is indeed good!" exclaimed Wakan Tanka. "Fawn need only lie still when Mother Deer is gone. The spots and lines will hide him. When I blew the colors dry, I blew his scent far away, too. Now he cannot be seen even by the eye of the Cougar or smelled by the nose of Wolf. Your little one is safe."

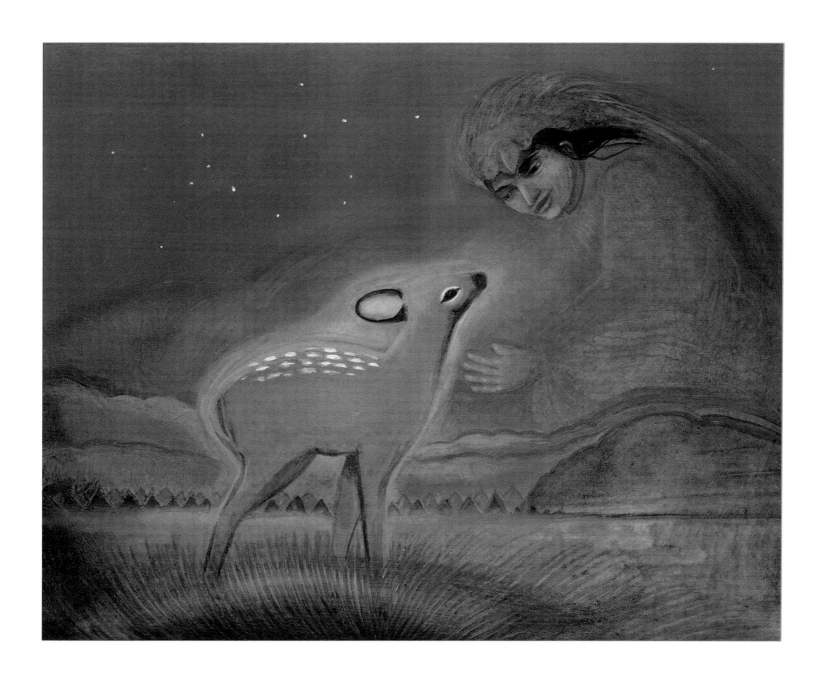

"But," Wakan Tanka went on, "all must have an equal chance and only that. I have given all my children many gifts, but I have given none of my children all gifts! As Fawn grows, he will be given new gifts. He will be given speed and strength. He will be given antlers and hooves to defend himself. It would not be fair to the other creatures if his spots still hid him or if he carried no scent to tell others where he was. So, as he grows strong and fast, the spots will leave and the scent will return. Then he will be matched equally against Wolf, Coyote, and Cougar. This is good," said Wanka Tanka.

And since that day, every fawn is born with spots to blend into the earth and without any scent to show its enemies where it hides. But when the fawn is old enough to receive the gifts of speed and strength, Wakan Tanka takes away the spots and gives it back its scent.

"It is good that you ask this," said the teacher around a campfire long since cold in a night long since passed. "Now you know that, like the fawn, you will receive different gifts as you grow older. You will develop speed like your brother. You will develop strength. But as you do, you will give up the gifts of childhood."

"It is good that you will know why the fawn has spots but not the deer. It is good that you know why these gifts have been given."

SOURCE NOTE:

This Story is adapted from one of the many Lakota (Sioux) Native American oral traditions surrounding creation and nature. Other versions of how the Fawn received its many gifts may be found in *Legends of the Mighty Sioux,* compiled by Workers of the South Dakota Writers Project, Work Projects Administration, published by Albert Whitman & Co., 1941. More complete studies of Lakota theology can be found in *Otokahekagapi (First Beginnings)* Sioux Creation Story, published by Tipi Press, 1987.

As with any oral tradition before the introduction of writing, many versions of this legend have been told and retold over the centuries. We hope you enjoy ours.

PRONUNCIATION NOTE:

Throughout, the Lakota name for the Creator has been used: Wakan Tanka, pronounced Wah-kon´ Tōn´-kah.